STEP INTO READING®

STEP 2

Oh My, Pumpkin Pie!

by Charles Ghigna

illustrated by Kenneth Spengler

Random House 🏠 New York

Autumn in the
pumpkin patch.
No two pumpkins
ever match!

See them growing
row by row.
Pumpkins put on
quite a show!

Pumpkins come
in many sizes.
Pumpkin shapes
are such surprises!

Pumpkins round
as basketballs.

Pumpkins flat
as old beach balls.

Pumpkins striped

in shades of yellow.

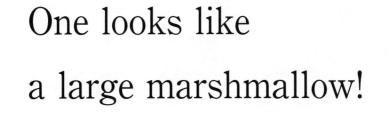

One looks like

a large marshmallow!

Some have bumps.

Some have none.

Some look like

a setting sun.

Some look like
a big balloon.

Some look like
a harvest moon.

Some look like

a spinning toy.

Some look like
a baby boy!

Pumpkins skinny.

Pumpkins fat.

Some look like
a tabby cat!

Some are shaped
just like a pear.

Some go to
the county fair!

Some BIG pumpkins
win a prize.

Some wind up
in pumpkin pies!

Pumpkin muffins!
Pumpkin bread!

One becomes

a scarecrow's head!

Pumpkin butter

on your toast.

Pumpkin seeds
are fun to roast!

What's the biggest
one you've seen?
Was it during
Halloween?

Looking friendly?

Looking mean?

With a smile

or with a scream!

Pumpkin faces
burning bright
in the cool
October night.